CINDERELLA

Hippo Books
Scholastic Publications Limited
London

Scholastic Publications Ltd, 10 Earlham Street, London WC2H 9LN, UK
Scholastic Inc, 730 Broadway, New York, NY 10003, USA
Scholastic Tab Publications Ltd, 123 Newkirk Road, Richmond Hill, Ontario, L4C 3G5, Canada
Ashton Scholastic Pty Ltd, PO Box 579, Gosford, New South Wales, Australia
Ashton Scholastic Ltd, 165 Marua Road, Panmure, Auckland 6, New Zealand

Text and illustrations, © The Mushroom Writers' & Artists' Workshop Ltd London 1986
Produced by Mushroom Books Ltd, London, for Scholastic Publications Ltd.
This edition © Scholastic Publications Ltd.
First published in the UK 1986.
Typeset by Centra Graphics Ltd, London. Origination FE Burman, London. Printed and bound by Mondadori, Italy.

Once upon a time there was a lovely young girl who lived with her widowed father. He had brought up his daughter alone and she had grown up kind and gentle as well as very beautiful. All went well until one day he decided to marry again. His second wife was the haughtiest woman that ever was, a widow with two ugly daughters. She had an evil temper matched only by the evil tempers of her daughters. From the start she hated her stepdaughter who was lovelier than her own girls, and of a far sweeter nature, too.

The wedding was a splendid affair with celebrations spread over several days. A great feast was laid on. People came from far and wide and there was singing and dancing late into the night. During this time the stepmother did her best to conceal her true feelings for her new daughter. No one guessed the hatred hidden in her heart. Then as soon as the ceremonies were over and the last guest had gone home, the stepmother wasted no time in showing her true nature. From dawn till dusk she made her stepdaughter iron gowns, polish shoes, clean stairs, scrub pots, sweep grates, darn stockings and wait at table.

In the mornings it was the poor girl's task to braid her stepsisters' hair, lace them into their corsets and help them into their gowns. And at night she helped them out of their gowns, unlaced their corsets and unbraided their hair. But still she had not finished. While the household slept there was coal to fetch, fires to be laid and the table to set for breakfast the following day.

The stepmother gave her two girls the finest rooms in the house. To her stepdaughter she gave the coldest attic room and the hardest bed covered with a quilt so thin it barely kept out the winter chill. To keep warm the poor girl had to sit in the kitchen in the chimney corner with her feet among the cinders. Because of this, her stepsisters gave her the name Cinderella. And so she was called.

Despite her cruel treatment not once did Cinderella complain. Instead she took comfort from her many animal friends: the white mice who lived behind the wainscotting in the kitchen; the fat toad who had made his home in the garden pond; and the lizards who lived in the dry stone wall which skirted the kitchen garden.

No creature was afraid of Cinderella, for they knew she was kind and gentle. When she was outside gathering fruit or cutting flowers, the birds flew down to eat from her hands and, at night, when she was in need of company, the mice came to her and curled up on her lap.

Although she loved these creatures Cinderella had no human friends, and she was very lonely. Even her father had no time for her any longer. Sitting in the chimney corner Cinderella would put her face in her hands and weep. Not even her friends the white mice could cheer her. It seemed that nothing could ease the wretchedness of her life.

It happened one day that a footman called at the house to deliver an invitation. Cinderella carried it into the room where her sisters were having breakfast.

"Ooh!" shrieked the elder sister. "What have you got there?"

Before Cinderella had a chance to answer, the letter was snatched from her hand and the seal was broken open.

"Oh goodness gracious! Oh my!" cried the elder sister.

"What is it?" demanded the other one.

"An invitation from the prince to attend a ball."

The younger sister jumped up with delight, crying, "A palace ball! Think of it!"

"Who is likely to attend the ball?" asked the younger sister, excitedly.

"The whole of society, I shouldn't wonder," came the reply. "There will be plenty of barons and earls, dukes and duchesses, and you and I, of course."

"Am I invited, too?" asked Cinderella, who had been standing in the doorway all the time.

"You!" cried the elder sister. "You invited to a ball at the palace!" She fell into great peals of laughter, which left her so breathless she had to ask for her corsets to be loosened.

The following days were taken up with preparations for the ball.

"I shall wear my new taffeta gown," announced the elder sister.

"And I shall wear my crêpe," said the younger, "for it makes me look so glamorous!"

Cinderella was kept very busy, pressing and starching clothes and waiting on her stepsisters. The day of the ball finally arrived, and the stepsisters rose early so that they would have plenty of time to prepare themselves. They squabbled continually over whose turn it was to use the looking glass. As the evening drew on, noses were powdered and repowdered, and rouge was applied in great quantity.

In all the bustle and excitement, poor Cinderella was completely forgotten except when she was given an errand to run.

"Help me with my hair," ordered the eldest sister.

"No, find my necklace first," said the younger of the pair.

"Hurry up, Cinderella," added the elder. "It would never do for us to be late for the ball."

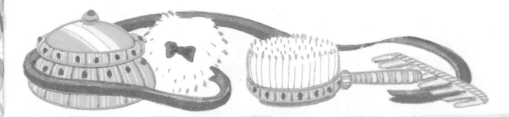

Eventually the coach arrived. There was a last minute panic when one of the sisters lost her fan and accused the other one of stealing it. But Cinderella quickly found the missing item beneath a cushion, and soon the sisters were stepping into the waiting coach.

"Must you take up so much room!" said the younger one, crossly, as she squeezed in beside her sister. "Move over, can't you?"

"Don't push," snapped the elder. "And careful you don't crease my gown!"

Then their differences were forgotten as the coachman urged his horses forward. "Don't wait up," they chorused to Cinderella, who stood waving on the drive.

She waved until they were out of sight. Then she went back to the kitchen. The house seemed strangely quiet after all the earlier bustle and excitement. Picking up the broom, she began to waltz slowly round the room imagining herself at the ball. For a moment she forgot her ragged clothes and worn shoes. Then suddenly she saw her reflection in the pots and pans hanging on the wall. She looked so silly!

Trying hard not to cry she stopped dancing and went to sit in the chimney corner. "How wonderful it would be to go to the ball," she sighed. But it was an impossible dream. She would have to content herself with hearing her sisters' account of the grand occasion.

"Don't cry, my child," said a gentle voice close to her shoulder.

She looked up and saw a beautiful stranger standing before her.

"Who are you?" asked Cinderella, unable to keep the surprise out of her voice.

"I am your fairy godmother," came the reply.

"But I didn't know I had one."

"Everyone has a fairy godmother," said the fairy. "Now dry your tears. Do you wish to go to the ball?"

"Oh, yes, please," cried Cinderella leaping up from where she sat.

"Then go you shall."

The fairy led Cinderella out into the garden. "Fetch me a pumpkin," she said, "the fattest, ripest one you can find."

Without stopping to ask what use a pumpkin could be, Cinderella skipped down to the vegetable patch. She hurried past the bean poles and rows of lettuce, past the asparagus bed and marrow clumps until she came to the place where the pumpkins grew. The first pumpkin she found was too small; the second pumpkin was not yet ripe; but the third pumpkin was perfect, being the fattest, ripest one of all. She carried it back to her godmother who scooped out the inside leaving only the rind.

"Stand back," said the fairy waving her magic wand. She tapped the pumpkin three times. At once it was transformed into a splendid gleaming coach.

Cinderella stood back in amazement. Then she clapped her hands crying, "But it's beautiful."

And it was indeed beautiful, being made of gold inlaid with rubies. There was just enough room inside for a princess to sit comfortably on the plump cushions.

"Go on," urged the fairy. "Step inside."

Cinderella opened the door of the coach and climbed inside. The curtains, she saw, were of the finest, heaviest brocade; the cushions were of the purest silk. "Can this be real?" she asked herself as she sunk down among them and looked out of one of the little windows.

"Comfortable?" asked the fairy.

"Oh, yes, thank you," replied Cinderella, who would have been content to stay there all night.

"We need horses," said the fairy.

She began to hunt about the garden, peering beneath leaves, looking behind large stones and poking her wand into clumps of plants. Cinderella followed close behind. Eventually she asked what they were looking for.

"White mice," replied the fairy. "They make the finest horses."

"Oh, but I know some white mice," said the girl, remembering her friends who lived behind the kitchen wainscotting.

The fairy told her to hurry and fetch six white mice.

Cinderella ran into the kitchen and called to her friends. A pink whiskered nose appeared from a hole in the wainscotting, then out tumbled a white mouse, then came another, then another until they were all over the place,

scampering around Cinderella, scrambling onto her lap and curling up among the folds of her dress. When they had quite tired themselves out Cinderella was able to explain that she needed their help. At once their excited squeaking started up again. They all wanted to help and Cinderella had been told by the fairy to choose only six; choosing between them seemed an impossible task.

The girl heard her fairy godmother calling her to hurry. Closing her eyes and pointing with her finger, Cinderella said, "I shall have you, you, you, you, you and you!"

As the six mice scampered outside the fairy tapped each one with her wand. In a twinkling they were transformed into handsome horses who pranced and capered and pawed the ground in their eagerness to be away.

The fairy told Cinderella that their work was not yet done. "A fine coach and handsome horses are all very well," she said, "but they are not much use without smart footmen. Though I have no idea where we are to find them at this time of night."

The fairy pondered for a moment then began searching round the garden once more. Cinderella almost had to run to keep up. Eventually she asked what they were looking for.

"Lizards," replied the fairy. "In my experience they make the smartest footmen."

Cinderella said that she knew some lizards who lived in the dry stone wall which skirted the kitchen garden.

"Run and fetch three of them," said the fairy. "Hurry now. There is no time to lose. You don't want to be late for the ball."

Cinderella hurried to the kitchen garden. Putting her face close to the wall she called to her friends. At the sound of her sweet voice a lizard darted out from between a crack in the stone. Then came two

more. Flicking their tails, they listened as Cinderella explained.

In an instant they had scrambled down the wall and were scurrying ahead of her across the lawn.

So swift were they it was almost impossible for the girl to keep up. She was quite out of breath by the time she reached the place where her godmother waited.

"Splendid, splendid," said the fairy looking approvingly at the lizards.

She tapped each one with her magic wand. At once they were changed into three smart footmen wearing gold jackets edged with braid, waistcoats the colour of emeralds and striped trousers. On their feet were polished shoes so shiny you could see your face reflected in them.

Cinderella could hardly believe it. They surely were the three smartest footmen she had ever seen.

Without wasting a moment the footmen went and took up their positions by the waiting coach.

Cinderella could hardly wait to be away but the fairy said one thing remained to be done.

"A fine coach, handsome horses and smart footmen are not much use without a coachman," said the fairy. "I don't suppose you have a friend who might help?"

"Well, as a matter of fact," began Cinderella, "I do know someone who would make a very jolly coachman."

"Bring him to me," said the fairy.

Cinderella ran to the garden pond. "Toad, toad," she called. "Are you there?"

The toad appeared from beneath a lily pad. The girl wasted no time asking him if he would be her coachman. In one bound he had leapt out of the pond and was hopping after her up the garden path.

The fairy nodded her head when she saw him. "Very satisfactory," she said, approvingly. She tapped him with her wand, and in an instant he was transformed into the fattest, jolliest coachman that was ever in charge of a coach. Leaping aboard he reined in the six handsome horses and called the footmen to order.

"Now you are ready to go to the ball," announced the fairy.

"Thank you, thank you," cried Cinderella, and she rushed to hug her godmother but the fairy had disappeared.

Cinderella called and called but there was no reply. Eventually she opened the door of the coach and stepped inside. As she sunk down among the cushions she suddenly caught sight of her shabby clothes.

"But I can't go to the ball like this," she cried. "I am dressed like a servant girl. They would not even let me into the palace kitchens!"

Fighting back her tears, Cinderella opened the door of the coach and stepped miserably down. The fine coach and the handsome horses, the smart footmen and jolly coachman were all for nothing. The poor girl would not be going to the ball after all…

She was about to trail miserably back to the kitchen when her godmother suddenly reappeared. She looked very flustered. "Forgive me, dear child," she cried. "Your gown! I forgot your ballgown!"

Gently she tapped Cinderella with her magic wand. The girl gasped - her old clothes disappeared and in their place was a ballgown of the finest silk, at her neck were pearls and on her feet were the prettiest pair of glass slippers she had ever seen. Now she was truly ready to go.

"Step into the coach, my dear." Cinderella did as her godmother said. "Before you leave I warn you of one thing. Do not stay later than midnight, for on the stroke of twelve your coach will turn back into a pumpkin, the footmen will be lizards once more, the coachman a toad and your clothes exactly as they were before."

Promising to leave before the magic hour, Cinderella commanded the coachman to urge his horses forward, and soon they were away.

In no time at all they arrived at the palace. The sound of music and laughter could be heard and through a window Cinderella saw fine ladies and gentlemen engaged in a stately waltz. Timidly she climbed the palace steps and entered the great oak doors.

She found herself in a brightly lit room filled with people. Imagine her surprise when the prince himself came forward to receive her! Bowing low he took her hand. The company fell silent as he led Cinderella on to the dance floor. Then a great hubbub broke out. "Who is she?" everyone cried. "What a beauty!" they said. "What hair, what eyes, what tiny feet!"

So taken was the prince with Cinderella he did not leave her side all night. But although he questioned her closely on where she came from and why they had never met before, she remained silent and refused to give away her secret.

Shortly the old king, who was as fascinated by the young princess as everyone else at the ball, demanded that she should be presented to him.

Curtseying low, Cinderella kissed the old man's hand. He told her to rise. "Sit by me for a while," he said. "I am too old to dance, but I never tire of charming company."

From the other end of the ballroom, Cinderella's stepsisters watched, never once guessing her identity.

"Isn't she lovely?" remarked the elder sister jealously.

"What a tiny waist!" said the younger one, who was almost green with envy.

"And what a charming smile. I wonder where she came from."

"Well, she's not from hereabouts that's for sure," announced the elder sister before going off to powder her nose for the eighteenth time that evening.

When the banquet was served, the prince insisted on sitting next to the princess. So intent was he on attending to her every need, he ate hardly a morsel. She had only to raise her eyes to his and he would invite her to take more glacé cherries, more figs, in fact more of everything that was on the sumptuous table. She was enjoying herself so much she had almost lost track of time. Then suddenly the clock struck eleven and three quarters. Remembering her godmother's words she rose from the table, curtsied to the assembled company, and hurried away.

The coach was outside the palace waiting to carry her home. When she reached home she found the fairy in the kitchen. Eagerly Cinderella began to recount what had passed at the ball. While she was doing so they heard her stepsisters returning.

"What a long time you have been!" cried Cinderella yawning and rubbing her eyes, as if she had been asleep all along and their arrival had only just woken her.

"You wouldn't have been asleep if you had been at the ball," said the elder sister, undoing her cloak and thrusting it into Cinderella's arms. "The most exquisite princess was there. Where she came from is a mystery. The prince had eyes for no one else."

"Yes," interrupted the younger sister, eager to prove that she too had seen the lovely princess. "No one in the room had a gown as gorgeous as hers. I intend to have one made up like it at the earliest opportunity."

"I doubt very much that a gown in that style would suit you," said the elder one cattily.

Before the two sisters could start arguing, Cinderella asked the name of the beautiful princess.

"No one knows her name," answered the elder sister. "It is said that the prince is very upset because she left so suddenly. He would give anything in the world to know who she was."

"How lucky you are to have seen her," said Cinderella. "Oh, do let me come with you to tomorrow's ball. Miss Charlotte, won't you lend me your yellow dress so that I might come with you?"

Miss Charlotte threw back her head and hooted with laughter. "You in my yellow dress at the ball! I would be a fool to lend anything to a grubby little Cinderella."

It was the answer Cinderella had expected and she smiled to herself. After she helped the sisters to bed she retired to her own tiny attic room, but she could not sleep. Her thoughts were only of the prince and the ball the following evening.

The next day when the sisters left for the ball, Cinderella followed soon after. She was dressed even more magnificently than before in a gown of shimmering gold. As she entered the ballroom the fine ladies and gentlemen drew back with admiring gasps, the band fell silent, and the prince came forward to meet her.

"I was afraid you would not come," he said. "May I have the first dance?"

For three waltzes the prince and Cinderella danced alone while the company stood back admiring her grace and elegance. Then gradually more and more couples took to the floor until the room was a kaleidoscope of swirling dresses and flashing jewels.

The prince insisted on dancing every dance with his princess. It was only when supper was announced that they paused for breath.

When the feast was over, Cinderella went to sit with her stepsisters but still they did not recognize her, though she was exactly the same kind, sweet girl who had done their hair only hours before.

Simpering and gushing they asked where she bought her fine clothes, whether she had any sisters and where she lived. They asked her age, the name of her dancemaster, and which fine balls she had attended in the past. In all they asked one hundred and one questions (though Cinderella answered none) and showed more interest in her in those few minutes than they had shown in all the time they had been sharing the same roof.

Eventually the prince could bear Cinderella's absence no longer. He came and claimed her hand and took her out on to the balcony to look at the stars.

Cinderella was enjoying herself so much she quite forgot the time. It was only when the clock struck twelve that she remembered her godmother's warning. She fled from the ballroom without a backward glance.

The prince hurried after her but she ran faster than he. As she sped down the steps her ballgown turned back into rags and she dropped one of her glass slippers. The prince picked it up.

"Have you seen a beautiful princess run past?" he demanded of the palace guard. But the guard replied that he had seen only a poor peasant girl pass by, and certainly no princess.

By the time Cinderella reached home she was cold and tired. For her coach had vanished along with her clothes. Her stepsisters arrived home soon after her. They were absolutely full of the ball.

"The beautiful princess was there," said the elder one. "She did us the very great honour of sitting with us for a while."

When Cinderella asked about the prince, the sisters told her that he was utterly besotted with the princess. "In her haste to leave the ball," explained the elder sister, "she left behind a glass slipper. The prince did nothing but stare at it for the rest of the night. He is in love, you mark my words!"

And she was proved right for the next day there was a royal proclamation. To the sound of trumpets it was announced that the prince would marry the girl whose foot fitted the slipper. A gentleman-in-waiting was sent to all corners of the kingdom and every princess and duchess and countess and lady tried the slipper but it fitted none of them.

Eventually it was the turn of the stepsisters. They fought over who should be allowed to try the slipper first. The elder sister won. She claimed it was by virtue of her age but in fact it was by virtue of her sharp elbows. No matter how hard she tried she could not squeeze her foot into the slipper. And neither could her younger sister.

Cinderella, who had been watching the proceedings and who recognized the slipper as her own, came forward. "May I be allowed to try it on?" she asked.

Her sisters laughed scornfully at her. "Don't be silly," they cried.

The gentleman-in-waiting stepped forward. He had orders to try the shoe on every young woman in the kingdom, and he had noticed that Cinderella was very beautiful. "If this young woman wishes to try the slipper then she shall," he said.

Sitting her down he placed the slipper on her foot; it fitted perfectly.

"But this is impossible," cried the stepsisters together.

"This is an outrage," stormed the stepmother. Then Cinderella pulled from her pocket the other slipper and put it on. As she did so her fairy godmother appeared and touched Cinderella with her wand. Immediately she was clothed in a gown even more beautiful than those she had worn before.

Now the stepsisters recognized the fine princess they had met at the ball. For a moment they were speechless; then they fell upon their knees begging to be forgiven for the nasty things they had said and done in the past. Cinderella embraced them and forgave them, telling them to love her always. Then the gentleman-in-waiting conducted her to the palace, where the prince was waiting.

When he saw her he was even more charmed than before, and two days later they were married. The streets were decorated with flags and flowers and there was rejoicing and celebration throughout the kingdom.

From that day forward
Cinderella and the prince
lived happily ever after.